TALES
OF
LIGHT AND DARK

Alex McGilvery

TALES OF
LIGHT AND DARK

Alex McGilvery

Copyright Alex McGilvery 2017
ISBN 978-1-7751286-4-9

HERO WANTED

"I am not a bad man." Lord Robert, the King's Sculptor said.

The Lord High Sculptor's companion, who was altogether unremarkable, nodded his head, not in agreement, but to convince the artist to get to the point. Give him a King or a merchant who would just say 'Go and kill so and so.'

"The King wants another statue for the Garden of Heroes." the sculptor said. "There are eight figures on the north side, and only seven on the south." Bob nodded again. "There are only fifteen great heroes in our tradition. We need to create a new hero."

"Why do you need me to make up a hero?"

"No, no, no. It must be an authentic hero. That is where you come in. You need to start a war. Not a big war, I don't want too much trouble, but enough of a conflict to allow someone to rise to the occasion. Go look at the Garden and you will see what I need."

Bob made his escape and visited the Garden of Heroes. He thought of himself as a hardened killer, but those statues turned his stomach. Each of the fifteen heroes was shown dying in extreme agony. One was being torn apart by huge wolves, another was filled with countless arrows. The worst part was that Bob began to see how he could accomplish the task.

***

The war with the trolls began through a series of tragic misunderstandings. A hunting party found itself on troll territory. It wouldn't have been so bad if the trolls hadn't taken all the horses to eat, or if the King's nephew hadn't been breaking in his favourite horse.

That incident might have been forgotten, if a party of trolls hadn't missed the boundary stones and wandered into the kingdom. Unfortunately, they bumped into the nephew who decided to find out whether trolls truly turned to stone in sunlight. They do.

Things went downhill from there.

***

Bob sat polishing his commander's boots. He was annoyed, so he was smiling. The war was rolling along, but in spite of all his maneuvering no heroes had risen to the occasion. Several soldiers had died, but none gruesomely enough or at an important enough point in the conflict. All Bob's efforts to push this new commander into heroics had failed. Lord Robert was getting impatient.

It was time for another move.

***

Bob cursed his stupidity. A border war was bad enough, but this was an all-out invasion. He sent a scout to warn the army, but it would be daylight before they arrived. Only one hope remained. There was stone bridge across a gorge that his squad might be able to hold. Killer he might be, but he didn't want to be ruled by trolls.

They refused to meet the strong but ungainly trolls head on. They tripped them and tangled their feet with rope. Bob and his crew fought through the night backing up inch by inch. One by one they fell. Finally, only Bob remained. In the gray dawn, he fell. As a troll roared in triumph and went to stomp on him, the sun rose. Petrified troll blocked the bridge.

***

The commander came to the Lord High Sculptor.

"Bob was a great hero, but he asked me to tell you he plans to die of old age in bed. I didn't understand until he explained everything."

Lord Robert paled as soldiers pulled up a troll frozen in mid stomp.

"The King thought the empty place could be filled with an object lesson."

STRAW INTO GOLD

Fiona lived with her parents in their little croft at the edge of a marsh. Every morning she'd comb out the wool from their sheep. Every afternoon she'd spin the wool into thread. Every evening she'd weave the threads into good wool cloth.

One day the Laird came riding up to the gate.

"Hello," the Laird called out. "I am looking for a good wool cloak. Fiona came out from her work and brought cool water from the well.

"I am sure Fiona will weave her best for you." Her father smiled and shooed her back into the croft. "She can weave gold from straw."

Well, the Laird's ears perked up. He had money needs of his own to be sure.

"I do need a new cloak, but I need gold even more." The Laird stood. "Bring her by the castle and we will see." He fixed Fiona's father with a fierce glare. "Do not disappoint me, or it will be worse for you."

When Fiona's father told her what he had done, she wept bitterly, but they were caught. In the morning, she walked down the road with eyes dry and mind working furiously. To get to the Laird's castle they had to pass by the black marsh. At lunch, she sat by the dark water.

"Foolish, foolish, foolish," she muttered. "Who would dream of weaving gold from straw?"

"Not so hard if you know the trick." a voice said from the water. Fiona started and looked around, but saw only rocks, trees, and her sleeping father.

"Would it be a trick that you could teach me?" Asked the girl.

"For a price." Said the voice. "It is an easy enough thing. Go on to the Laird's castle and I will come to you there."

Fiona continued to the Laird's castle. She arrived in the evening, and was shown into a cold room with a hard mat on the floor. In the morning, a servant came and took Fiona to a room filled with straw. The Laird waited for her at the door.

"If you can weave this into gold, well and good. If not..." He shrugged and left, locking the door behind him.

Fiona looked at the room and felt her heart sink. It just wasn't possible.

"Foolish, foolish, foolish," she muttered. "If you are here, I could use your help."

"Close your eyes," the voice said. She closed them tight, and a gentle hand led her to a chair. "Take the comb, and comb at the straw, but see in your mind the finest wool. But you must keep your eyes closed the whole day."

"What is the price for your help?" Fiona asked.

"The merest trifle." Whispered the voice. "Just a kiss."

Fiona tilted her head up and felt the brush of lips across her own.

All day she combed the straw as if it were the finest wool with her eyes tight closed. Just as the light faded, the voice whispered.

"Open your eyes." The room was filled with the finest wool all combed and cleaned.

"Where is the gold?" the Laird demanded, his eyes dark.

"You see wool where you had straw," Fiona said. "Can you not be content?"

A servant took her back to a chamber with a fire and soft mattress.

The next morning, she was taken back to the room.

"Today I want to see gold." the Laird pushed into the room and slammed the door.

"Foolish, foolish, foolish," Fiona whispered. "If you are here I could use your help."

Once again the voice instructed her and led her with eyes shut to the chair. Once again the hand was gentle and the kiss a mere brush of lips. Again, Fiona worked, eyes closed, spinning the wool into thread. And again, as the last wool came off the wheel, the Laird burst into the room.

"Where is the gold?"

"You see thread where you had straw. Can you not be content?"

"If I see gold tomorrow," the Laird said, "I will marry you."

The servant led her to a fine suite with a bath and meal laid out. Yet Fiona lay awake all night. In the morning when she was brought to the room, she walked to the chair and began weaving at the loom. All day with her eyes open she weaved thread into good wool cloth. Just as the last light was leaving the room, she closed her eyes and whispered.

"If you are here, I would speak with you."

"I am here." Whispered the voice.

"What happens if I open my eyes?" Fiona asked.

"Then I must leave you forever." the voice whispered.

"Then I will keep my eyes closed, but I want to go with you."

"Do you not want to marry the Laird?"

"I would rather a gentle hand and loving kiss."

The gentle hand led her out of the room, out of the castle to the edge of the marsh.

"Kiss me." the voice said.

She kissed him, with lips and heart together.

"You may open your eyes." She saw a figure before her, not quite a man, not quite anything else.

"What do I call you?" Fiona asked.

"I am the Glothogach."

"Then I will be the Glothogach's wife." Fiona took his hand.

"What of the Laird?" the Glothogach asked.

"If he can't make gold out of good wool cloth, he isn't much of a Laird."

RED HAT

The small group huddled around their tiny campfire. Though the rain had stopped the temperature plummeted. Dwarves are a hardy bunch, but the combination of cold damp weather and lack of success prospecting for new ores made these ones as miserable and short tempered as any thin blooded human.

"We're going to be out of wood before the night is out." the one with the longest beard said. "Red Hat, go and fetch some more."

"Oh sure, I would love to haul myself back down the mountain to pick up a few sticks, then climb back up in the dark. I told you to put some in your packs, but no, you're too high and mighty to carry firewood." The red hatted dwarf pulled his hat tighter about his ears and hunched closer to the fire.

"You're a dwarf, you can see in the dark." another dwarf nudged him ungently with her foot. "You're wearing the red hat; you go get firewood."

"You didn't tell me that when you gave me the hat." the hat wearer grumbled. "You just said it would keep me warm."

"Well, you'll be warm enough going down the mountain." One of the other dwarves said. "We all took our turns wearing the red hat."

Muttering under his breath the youngest dwarf stood up and started back along the path. He had got as far as the rock face with the odd vein running through it when a loud crack startled him. He peered around hoping it was a stick that he had dropped. All he saw were flakes of rock on the path. There was another crack and a flake fell to the ground in front of him. He looked up the rock face to see where it had come from.

"Hey," he yelled. "Come look at this."

"Wood, Red Hat," The other dwarves yelled. "Go get some."

"No, there's a hand coming out of the rock." The dwarves around the fire made derisive noises.

He stumped back to the fire and grabbed the only remaining long piece of burning wood. The others tried to grab him but he ran back to the rock-face.

"See look, in that black vein." He waved his makeshift torch. The others crowded around him, the cold forgotten.

"It's moving."

The hand was as large as their heads, and it opened and closed, twisted and contorted. Each time it moved, more rock would fall to the ground. Gradually it became clear of the rock. They watched as huge rough fingers gripped the rock and strained as if to pull the rock back in. But it wasn't pulling rock in, it was pulling something out. Soon they could see a thick wrist then a forearm. Each time it pulled it had a longer reach. Soon the arm up to the elbow stuck out of the rock. It bent and they could see sinews bunch and move in effort. The rest of the arm and a shoulder appeared.   Another massive heave and a rock the size of Red Hat popped out of the vein. It shook itself and roared.

"Oh slag heaps," one of the dwarves moaned. "It's a troll."

The troll rolled its head on its shoulders while flakes of rock fell from its face. Its eyes opened and it saw the dwarves. Quicker than they thought possible it snatched at the group. They jumped back stumbling over each other. The troll's hand waved a dwarf's red hat about.

"Great, now my ears are cold." He darted forward and waved the torch in the troll's face, but with a huge crack the other arm popped out of the rock and almost captured the young dwarf. With a squeak, he scuttled away. Head and shoulders free, the troll began to heave the rest of itself out of the rock.

"It is time we were going." the oldest dwarf said. "We don't want to be here when it gets clear of that cliff." The others looked at him and jogged back to the remains of their fire. In minutes, they had packed up their gear and headed along the trail back down the mountain. The troll's arm snaked out and grabbed Red Hat's backpack. He wormed out of it just before the troll pulled him back to the rock. His companions pulled him out of the way before the other hand could grab him. They headed the other way up the trail.

Red Hat was in the back trying to keep up with a twisted ankle. The troll would pull the rest of itself free of the rock. Then, hungry from its efforts, the troll would chase after the dwarves to crush them and eat them. Maybe if he slowed down it would give the others time to get away.

"Keep up. I haven't lost a Red Hat yet, and I won't start tonight." The oldest dwarf passed his mountain stick back to the young dwarf.

"Here, this way." called the lead dwarf. "Careful though." They crept out across a snowfield. By now the troll was close behind them, but its much greater weight caused the snow to give way and with a final roar it disappeared down the mountain.

"When I was Red hat," the oldest dwarf. "I put a dragon's egg on the fire"

Huddled together. the dwarves told stories 'till dawn.

20

SWAN BROTHERS

If my Da had any fault it was he boasted too much about his sons. My brothers were kind when they thought of it, but mostly they never noticed me.

One day a Queen came to see these fine lads. As fair and chill as diamonds she was. I met her at the door. I who was never a part of my Da's boasting, being but a daughter.

The Queen walked into our hut and looked at each of my brothers straight in the eye, and each, from oldest to youngest dropped their gaze before her.

I offered her tea and sat her at our rough table. Seeing our visitor well seated, and likely well drowned by my chatter, my brothers went back to what they do best. That is to talk about what they would do when the world was right and they were rich as kings.

I saw the first storm cloud cross the fair brow of that Queen. She wasn't pleased to be left to a chattering girl while the men ignored her. Queens aren't used to being ignored.

She stood up abruptly and set the dishes to clattering. I saw the storm darken and lightening ready to strike.

"Please, O Queen," I begged, "Don't hurt them."

"These are your sons?" she asked my father in her cold voice. "I don't see much to boast of." My seven brothers looked up, only now aware of their danger, but all too late. She waved her hand at them and they fell to the ground. Feathers covered them. Before I could take a breath, they had been changed into swans. In a rush my brothers flew out the door leaving only my Da with his mouth hanging open, the Queen with darkness still flashing from her eyes, and seven white feathers lying by the hearth.

"What have I done?" my father moaned as he threw himself at her feet.

"You have been foolish, as only mortal men can be foolish," replied the Queen. "Now only one thing may repair your boasting." She looked at me.

My father stared at me then at the Queen.

"Her?"

"Her."

The Queen came over and took me by the chin and looked deep into my eyes, indeed into my very soul.

"If Meg here stays silent for seven years, she might restore her brothers. She must sew each of them a shirt from the nettles that grow upon the hills." She looked at me again, "You must pick the nettles, spin the thread, and weave the cloth with your own hands. Not a whisper or a sigh may pass your lips."

I opened my mouth, then closed it again. She nodded at me and touched my lips with a finger, then vanished.

I once woke with words already on my lips, and fell asleep with my sentence unfinished. Now a rock was not more silent than I. My Da would rise in the morning and look at me, then lie himself back down again. He took himself off to join Ma in heaven before the end of the first year.

I wandered the hills to gather nettles. I bit my lips against letting a whimper out as they stung. My hands were soon red and swollen. In the evenings, I would pound the bitter stalks until they split and I could spin thread from them. The thread I tied on a loom my Ma had left me and wove into cloth. That was my life for six years.

In the seventh year, a young man came to our village. He was near as quiet as I had become, helping neighbour and friend. Of course, he came to see me. I was the village boast now. Mad Meg, who hadn't made a sound in six years. They made a game of it, trying to trick me into speech. All failed.

Bran came to watch me weave. He talked softly of his day, while I sent the shuttle flying back and forth on the loom. I was working on the cloth for the last shirt - for my little brother. So the days passed, and Bran fell in love with Mad Meg, and I with him. He poured his heart out to me begging for a word of love. I stayed silent, and the day before seven years was done, he walked out of my house.

Seeing his back disappear down the road I came closest to breaking my silence. Still, I let my heart break in silence.

At last the morning it waited for came, and I took the shirts and the feathers outside to wait. Seven swans came with the smallest a bit behind. I cast the shirts over their heads. As each one returned to himself, he would look at me and shake his head, then go into the house.

The last one, the shirt was too small. I had forgotten how even little brothers grow. I left him with one arm and one wing. I crumpled and wept silent tears into the dust. My brother lifted me up.

"Thank you, Meg." He whispered. "I saw a man with sad eyes on the road." He pointed with his wing. "I am thinking you need him more than we need you."

I gave him a hug and ran off away to find my love.

My first words would be his.

ALBERT

Once upon a time there lived a frog named Albert. Albert was quite content as a frog. He had his lily pad, his friends and a wonderful voice. Everybody knows that frogs are great singers, but Albert's voice was something special. Whenever he sang the whole pond would stop and listen to him sing. Albert sang about the moon shining on the pond at night, about sleeping warm in the mud through the winter and about bathing in the warm light of the sun. It was in fact, Albert's voice that got him into trouble.

In a castle, up on a hill, overlooking
Albert's pond, lived a King and his family. The
royal family lived content, with the exception
of the youngest daughter whose name was
Sue. Where princesses were supposed to be
graceful and composed, Sue was somewhat
ungainly and terribly shy. Somehow she never
acted quite like a princess should. Her brothers
and sisters taunted her unmercifully. Even the
servants in the castle teased her.

One spring evening when the air was
especially still she stood on the balcony of her
room listening to the sounds of the spring
night. Since her room overlooked the pond,
she of course heard Albert singing.

"Even a frog has something special that
makes him sing so beautifully." She sighed and
leaned her head against the cool glass. "I wish
I knew what that frog is singing about so
wonderfully. She shook her head. "What
nonsense I am thinking tonight to envy a frog
his voice." She turned to go into her room.
Just as she was closing the doors behind her
she heard a beautiful bass voice singing of the
joy of spring under the first star of the night.
Transfixed the princess stood and listened to
the velvety voice.

"O dear me, you will catch your death of cold."

Sue jumped and turned to her nurse.

"You startled me." She closed the doors and came into the room. she stretched and gave a tremendous yawn. "I'm so tired."

"Such a yawn for a princess." Her nurse clucked and helped her change for sleep. "It isn't at all becoming."

Sue blushed and climbed into her bed. When the light was out and she was alone, Sue lay awake and stared at the ceiling.

"Why do I need a nurse anyway? I've grown far beyond the age I need a nurse." Still grumbling she drifted off to sleep.

The next morning did not begin well. First, Sue was late for breakfast. her mother glared as Sue hurriedly slid into her seat and sent the juice glasses to slopping over onto the white tablecloth.

"Oh, I am sorry, I slept late." Sue mopped at the juice with her napkin.

"My dear, you are a princess," the Queen said, "you must be punctual. If you cannot be on time, don't make excuses, and certainly don't rush about out of breath."

After breakfast the princesses gathered to work on their needle point. Sue stabbed herself, and bled so badly that she ruined three months of painstaking work. Her finger bandaged, she was sent outside to amuse herself until lunch, with the order to stay out of the mud, and her sisters' demure titters ringing in her ears.

What use is it to be a princess if I can't be a happy princess? Gradually the warm sun began to cheer her up. Then she heard the wonderful voice from the night singing. Following the voice until she reached the pond Sue saw a large green frog sitting on a stump. She squealed and jumped back. The frog jumped into the pond. The ball which the princess dropped, rolled into the pond.

"How am I going to get my ball back without getting covered with mud?" the princess wailed. "Oh, why can't I do anything right?"

***

Albert looked carefully out from under the water. The girl sat on the grass crying bitterly. He had often seen the princesses playing near his pond and felt sorry for the youngest princess. He liked her best because she was the only one who ever seemed to appreciate his pond. On an impulse, he dived down into the water and with a great effort pushed the ball to the surface and rolled it to the princess. Sue looked at him in astonishment.

"Thank you, oh, thank you." She grabbed the ball and laughed. "They will never believe this in the castle." Albert was so pleased with himself that he swelled up with song. Sue's eyes bulged and she almost dropped her ball again.

"It was you singing last night." She gasped in astonishment. "You must be a prince under enchantment. no frog could sing so beautifully." The princess looked around. "I will take you home and break your enchantment. Then we can be friends." She quickly caught Albert and ran home to hide him in her room.

Albert was devastated. This place was cold and hard, and worst of all it was dry. There not a decent bit of water or mud to be found. He missed the sun and the familiar murk of his pond. As the day turned into evening his loneliness became so great that he began to sing. It was a terribly mournful song, and as

Sue came into her room and heard it, it caught at her heart.

"It must be terrible to be a prince, and have to live as a frog." She picked Albert up and hugged him. Albert was so sad that he kept singing his unhappy song. "Frog." Sue said between her sobs, "You are so unhappy. I wish I could make you a prince." And she kissed him.

"Who is that man? the King thundered from the doorway. Sue didn't answer, for she was staring at Albert in amazement. Albert had turned from a frog into a man.

"Why are you in my daughter's bedroom?" The King roared at Albert, but Albert didn't answer either he was looking at himself in amazement.

"Why frog, you are a prince." Sue squeaked.

"Hardly a prince if he appears like that in a princess's bedroom." the King bellowed, since, being a frog, Albert had no clothes.

The King and Queen were up all night discussing what they were going to do. They finally decided that the only way to avoid a scandal was for Albert and Sue to get married, immediately, so they planned the wedding for the next week.

Albert found the change to palace life very difficult. He wasn't sure how to eat with knife and fork. Clothes were strange and uncomfortable. But most of all he missed being a frog and singing in his beloved pond all day. The only thing that made it at all bearable was the princess. She taught him how to eat with utensils and helped him choose the most comfortable clothes. She even stood up for him when he chose his entire wardrobe in green. But each evening Albert would slip out of the castle and go down to the pond. There he would sit in the light of the moon and sing. They were sad songs, and Sue listening on her balcony would determine to try even harder to make her prince happy.

One day while Albert and Sue sat in the sunny courtyard escaping from the wedding plans for a brief time Sue's nurse came out to bustle Sue back into the castle.

"I'm about to be married. I don't need a nurse." Sue yelled in rebellion. "Go away, and don't bother me anymore." The old woman looked at Sue then slowly and silently left.

"Why did you yell at her so?" Albert asked. "Surely she is only trying to help."

"She's been my nurse longer than I can remember. But I don't need a nurse anymore, and I don't like being fussed over."

"If you don't need a nurse, maybe she needs you." Sue looked at him quizzically.

"Why should she need me. I'd think that she would be glad to do something else for a change."

"What?" Albert asked reasonably. "She has always been Nurse."

"I don't know. That's her problem anyway." Sue grumped.

"You are her princess. I think that makes it your problem." Albert pointed out. "You should give her something else to do if you want her to stop bothering you."

Sue looked at him for a moment.

"I hadn't thought of that." She jumped up. "I'm going to go and talk to her."

"What are you going to ask her to do." Asked the frog prince.

"To be the nurse for our children!" Sue laughed, and ran off to find Nurse. Albert sighed and wandered down to the pond. He thought wistfully of his old uncomplicated life as a frog.

Yet as the days before the wedding shortened, Albert's common sense made itself felt. Even the King found himself discussing difficult problems with his guest. The Queen went so far as to admit one night while she and the King worked over the proclamation for the wedding that Albert might make quite a suitable match.

"By the way dear, have you found out exactly who Albert is?" She asked. "We really can't have a proclamation reading 'Today the Princess Susan Aurelia Constance Esther marries Albert.' We need to know a little more about his background."

"Quite right, you should ask Sue in the morning."

The next morning, the day before the wedding, Sue walked down the stairs to breakfast.

"Good morning." She smiled, and glided into her place.

"Good morning Sue." The Queen nodded. "Your father found a minor detail that needs to be cleared up. We need to know Albert's full name and a little more about him for the proclamation."

"I have been so busy that I never thought to ask him." Sue said. "I will ask him today."

Out in the courtyard, which had become their favourite place, Sue found Albert. He was staring moodily through the gate down toward his old pond.

"Albert, my mother asked me what your other names are."

"Other names? I only have one name."

"But Princes always have lots of names. Like me, I have four."

"I like Sue best," Albert said with a smile.

"But you are a Prince, you must have other names."

"No." Albert sighed "I have no other names. I am not a Prince." Susan stared at him, then laughed.

"You must be a Prince. Why would anyone enchant somebody who wasn't a Prince?"

"You did, Sue." Albert said looking at her with an expression she couldn't quite fathom.

"Oh Albert." Sue blushed.

"But you did Sue. You turned me into a Prince."

"And if I turned you into a Prince, what were you before?" She demanded.

"A frog. I'm a frog Sue. I was never a prince until I met you."

"You're not an enchanted Prince?" Sue's face turned red. "You let me think you were a Prince all this time, and all the time you were just a frog? What am I going to tell my father? That I'm marrying a frog?" Sue stood now, screeching at him.

Albert flinched with each question.

"You creature. You abominable creature. I hate you." The princess turned and fled from the courtyard.

Albert sat for a long while, then slowly he stood and walked down to the pond, a sad, shrinking figure in green.

•••

The Princess locked herself in her bedroom. She refused to talk to anyone. Other than to tell her father through the door that the wedding was off; that everything had been a terrible mistake. She closed the window then wept on her bed for three days.

Finally, she got up and washed her face. Squaring her shoulders, she unlocked the door and went down to breakfast. Her family greeted her with a wary silence. The Queen gave her an approving nod.

Things returned almost to normal. As the weeks passed, Sue floated quietly through life, her face cold and pale. She rapidly lost weight. One morning she no longer had the strength to get up.

The King and Queen worried about her. They begged their daughter to tell them what was making her so unhappy. But Sue simply stared out the window and said nothing. The old nurse came to the princess's room to be by her side. She bustled about cleaning and tidying, opening the window to let the fresh summer air in. The day passed and as the evening came Sue heard a voice singing outside her window. It sang of the summer night, and the sorrow of a love lost. It sang of the moon shining on the pond and of a beautiful princess named Sue. It sang of enchantment and a broken heart.

"Albert," the princess whispered. She stood and staggered to the window. "Albert."

His deep, sad voice soared through the night,

　　telling of the joy and sorrow of his love.

Sue sat on the balcony and listened to the song through the night. In the grey of the early morning she slipped out of the castle. Walking slowly but with iron determination she made her way down to the pond.

"Albert." She called into the silver mists. "Albert, I'm sorry. I love you." The effort of walking overcame the weakened princess and she fainted beside the pond. There Albert, once again a frog, found her.

"My poor Sue." Albert said as he kissed her. "I wish I could make you happy."

The rising sun shone gold on two happy frogs as, hand in hand, they hopped into the pond.

JACKS

Queen Gillian sat at the oak table in her council chamber and played at jacks while her advisors argued amongst themselves. She was young to be Queen - not yet a decade, but her father had died in the same plague that had devastated the male population of her kingdom.

"I say that we muster our troops and meet them at the border. We will push them into the river or die trying."

"We don't have enough men to hold the border. We must pull back and prepare the castle for a siege."

Jill finished her eightsies and put the jacks and the ball away.

"We have lost enough men to the plague," the young Queen said, "We will not throw any more lives away. This is what we will do."

***

Prince Johan rode at the head of his army of unwanted extra sons from his land.

"General, send a reminder down the line. There will be no looting or molesting the people. If we plan to live here we must not make enemies of my future subjects." The older man nodded and signalled his staff. The Prince led his army across the river.

They rode without resistance through a countryside rich with fields ready for harvest. They arrived at the city gates to find them wide open and a Marshall on a white horse waiting for them. He carried a white flag on a standard.

"My Queen would meet with you and your General," he said, "The rest of your men are welcome to make camp on the pasture."

"Give the orders," Johan said.

They followed the Marshall through a city with far too few men. The people's eyes followed the invaders with an expression the Prince couldn't name – somewhere between despair and hope.

Queen Gillian met them in her council room.

Prince Johan bowed deeply to the young girl in front of him. She was dressed in the simplest of frocks, and only a gold wire holding back her hair hinted at royalty.

"As I am sure you are aware Prince Johan, my kingdom has suffered deeply. We need the men that you have brought with you to rebuild. The question then is who will rule this Kingdom?" the Queen walked over to the Prince and looked him long and hard in the eyes. "My people would not be content to be ruled by a foreign prince."

"You don't have the means to stop me from taking the throne."

"No, I don't," the Queen admitted, "But if I were to just give you the throne, what authority would you have to order your new Kingdom? I won't let you just walk in and take my Kingdom."

Prince Johan sighed. "I was hoping to avoid bloodshed."

"Nothing comes without a price." She upended a leather bag on the table and steel jacks clattered onto the oak. The ends of the jacks had been filed to sharp points. "Play me a game of jacks for my Kingdom. Let the only blood to be shed be yours and mine. If you win, the Kingdom is yours. If I win you will serve the Kingdom as I see fit."

"You would decide the fate of your kingdom with a child's game?"

"I'm a child."

"I used to be a fair hand at jacks," Johan said with a shrug.

"We each will get three tries. but first you must swear on the breath in your lungs and the salt in your veins. Swear on your mother's life and your father's grave, that you will abide by the outcome of the game."

Johan swore and the Queen did as well. She pushed the jacks and the ball to him.

"You start."

He tossed the ball in the air and picked up a jack. He breezed through the early rounds as his hands remembered the rhythm. Halfway through fours a sharpened jack stabbed deep into his finger. He gasped and missed the catch.

The Queen tossed the jacks and began playing. She made it to fives before a jack stuck in her hand. She caught the ball and pulled the jack out. She made it to sevens before missing a jack. She pushed the bloodied jacks to Johan.

He tossed them out and started at fours. This time he made it to sevens before missing the catch. The Queen almost immediately sent an errant jack spinning across the table. Johan started again, his hand was bleeding from tiny wounds and he had a hard time catching the now slippery ball, but he made it to nines before missing.

The Queen took her lip in her teeth. Her smaller hands were in worse shape than Johan's but she made it through nines to tens. Johan caught the ball on the next toss.

"You have won, my Queen."

The Queen took his hand in hers and led him into the throne room. A smaller chair sat beside the throne. She sat Johan in the chair.

"You and I will rule this land together." She kissed him on the cheek before seating herself and whispered to him. "I won't always be a child, my Prince."

What have I got myself into? Johan watched his General kneel to pledge allegiance to Queen Gillian.

ANYTHING FOR GOLD

Sascha limped into the bar and took a table where she could sit with her back to a wall facing the door. A young girl came and deposited a mug of beer on the table. Sascha used a scrap of sleeve wetted with beer to clean the blood from her face. The girl appeared again and left a cleaner cloth. Shascha smiled thanks and went back to her ablutions. She drank what was left of the beer and settled in for a long wait.

A polished steel shield hung on the wall. From what she could see of the bartender in it he looked more troll than human. Sascha

wondered what he thought of her. She knew
even with her best efforts, blood caked in her
eyebrows and hair, turning fiery-red dark.
Fortunately, none of the cuts and tears in her
clothes were in places which could cause
trouble.

Well after moonrise, Jacko slid into the
seat across from her. The room had filled up
and they could talk under the boisterous
crowd.

"What happened to you?"

"A couple of bravos thought they needed
my purse more than I did."

Jacko winced, "Did you have to let them
bleed all over you?"

"One thought he could hold me while his
partner finished me. I had to cut his throat."
She shrugged. "It was messy.

"They must have been desperate."

"I wouldn't know."

"After all that you didn't even check their
purses?"

"Whatever else I might be I am not a
thief."

"You could have taken enough for some
new clothes."

Sascha stared at him until Jacko looked down.

"OK, OK, you'll do anything for gold but steal it. I don't get you, Sasch."

"You don't need to get me." She leaned forward across the stained wood of the table. "Did you get the information I asked you about?"

"I did, the old man's holed up in the old monastery outside the south wall."

"Thanks" She dropped a handful of coins on the table. "Buy yourself a decent meal."

Her stained and ragged clothing helped Sascha blend into the shadows well enough the guards didn't notice her climb over the south wall. The moon shone bright enough to reveal handholds, but not so bright as to make her stand out. She reached the bottom and stretched out the cramps in her hands.

The place was more ruin than monastery. Walls and roofs now jumbles of stone. The only building still standing was the crypt for the monks who never left their retreat even in death. She pushed on the door and found it barred from the inside. She smiled, neither corpses or ghosts had any reason to bar the door. With the blade of her thinnest knife she lifted the bar and eased the door open.

The faint gleam of moonlight didn't show anything but dust and bones. She entered the crypt and followed the faint scent of cheese. An old man waited for her.

"Robson sent you."

"He wants the stone."

"Ah," the old man nodded. "Want some cheese?"

Sascha shrugged and took the chunk of cheese from his hand. She bit into it and almost cried at its sharp flavour against her tongue.

"There is water if you wish to clean up." He tossed her a bundle of cloth. "My fellows won't mind if you borrow a robe. The smell of death disturbs me."

"You're afraid of dying?" Sascha asked through the splashes of water on her face.

"No."

"I was hoping you would be."

"So I would just give you the stone?"

"I don't want to kill you."

"But you will if you have to."

"I will do what I need for Gold."

The old man looked at her sadly.

"I don't see greed in your eyes."

"Nonetheless."

He reached into his robe and pulled out a tiny bundle wrapped in silk.

"Silk is the only substance that the stone won't affect. Be careful." He handed it to her.

Sascha allowed the silk to move from the stone and touched it against a bone that lay on the floor. It turned into pure yellow gold.

"Why?"

"You are at the very edge of darkness. I didn't want to push you over."

"Then you understand."

"Goodbye Sascha, you're almost free."

"Without Gold, I will never be free."

"Remember the silk." The crypt went dark.

Sascha found herself outside the crypt. She shook her head and patted the small weight of the stone in her pocket.

***

Robson was waiting for her in the room he called his throne room.

"You have it?"

"Gold first."

He snapped his fingers and one of the thugs beside him pulled a little girl from behind Robson; her hair the colour fine gold.

"Mommy!" the girl cried.

"Hi Gold."

Robson took the little girl's hand and kept her from running to her mother.

"The stone first."

"This is the last time," Sascha said holding up the tiny bundle.

"Sascha, Sascha, you can trust me. Let me see the stone, then we'll talk." He let go of Gold and the girl ran to her mother.

Sascha tossed the stone to Robson and swept up Gold in her arms. She used the bit of silk to wipe the tears from her daughter's eyes.

HONOUR

Sir Cathvart reined in his horse at the bridge. He held up his mailed fist to signal the rest of his troop to stop. Standing on the bridge was a man in rusty armour, but holding a well-kept sword.

"Out of my way. I am on a mission for the King."

"You may not pass."

"Come now," the knight dismounted and walked toward the man on the bridge, "We are both honour bound to obey the King's desires."

"Honour is a lie."

"Honour is everything. It is our honour as knights that makes us who we are."

The other man remained silent. Sir Cathvart could see that he was an older man, but there were remains of heraldic colours on his armour.

"We will have a test of arms. If you prevail, then my men will turn away and not bother you anymore. You hear?" he called, "If this good knight wins the day, then you are to pass by without molesting him. There. They will obey as men of honour."

The older man's answer was to lunge, quick as a snake. The point of his sword scraped across the paint of Cathvart's chest plate. Cathvart threw himself backwards but he rolled to his feet with sword in hand.

The rusty knight might have been older, but he was no slower or frailer than Sir Cathvart himself. After his first precipitate lunge, he followed up with several double handed blows that would have cleaved in a helm even if Cathvart were wearing one. The younger knight was able to push the blows to one side, but he wasn't able to set himself solidly.

He was forced back onto the road where his men had to scramble to get their horses out of the way. Finally, the old knight over extended just slightly, but Cathvart stepped aside and pushed him off balance. The knight stumbled to one knee. Cathvart stepped back and waited for the older man to right himself.

"You fight well."

"For an old man."

"I mean you fight well. You should come to the tourney. You would do well in the lists."

"I don't fight for fun." The older man began his attack again, but this time Cathvart was ready for him. Blows that would have split his armour open were pushed to the side. He saw an opening and tried an attack of his own. The rusty armour turned his blade and he leapt back to be ready for the next onslaught. The older man surprised him by chuckling and switching to a more subtle fencing style.

Now his sword came at him in feints and lunges that were much harder to parry than the graceless pounding that had started the fight. Cathvart found himself giving ground again.

"You are a strong fighter." Cathvart gasped, "Join our quest."

"And what is it this time? The horns from a golden cow? The hair of a mermaid?"

"You mock us." Cathvart managed to lock their swords for a brief moment. "The King is bringing peace to all the land. He will rule through his knights. They will rule with honour."

The older knight pushed him away and came very close to taking Cathvart's head.

"I told you," the old man said. "Honour is a lie."

The two knights circled on the road. While the older knight had a seemingly endless repertoire of attacks and feints, the younger knight was stronger and well trained. The mounted troop watched and occasionally hissed or cheered. On the other side of the bridge some peasants had heard the sound of battle and come to peer through the bushes to watch.

Both men were gasping for air now and their blows more often wide of their target. There was no more conversation. A strap on Sir Cathvart's right greave broke and the plate protecting his leg dangled lose. As he stepped back to adjust it he realized that the other man was going to strike at his vulnerable leg. It wasn't so much a plan as instinct which put his sword where it would catch the old knight's arm as he struck.

The blade sliced through the leather armguard and the rusty-armoured knight's sword fell to the dust.

"Well fought, but now you must let us pass." Cathvart let exhaustion pull his sword point down.

The old man swept up his sword with his left hand and ran through Cathvart's unprotected leg.

"I told you," the old man snarled, "I don't fight for fun." He tried to pull the sword out and finish the younger knight, but the steel was jammed in the powerful muscle of the thigh. That second of hesitation was enough for Cathvart's sword to find the man's throat.

Cathvart looked at the man he had killed.

"He was a strange man, but he died with honour."

"What should we do with them?" his lieutenant asked, pointing at the peasants.

"They are on the King's land. Kill them all."

Cathvart sat while his surgeon bandaged his leg. He wished he could join his troop in clearing the King's land. There was no honour in killing peasants, but it was practice of a sort. Instead he had to sit here and just listen to the screams.

LEARNING HONOUR

I was once where you are; watching the words go up into the blue like so many soap bubbles. You feel no care, no urgency, but be warned! in the right hands even soap bubble might be dangerous.

You say the words are floating to no purpose, your attention is fleeting, and there is a limit to how many words I have to tell my story?

Sadly, you are right, the days of the garrulous old narrator are past, so we start.

One of the times that I was young, Yes, I mean exactly that, I have been young many times; young as a flower, young as a tree, even young as a rock. This time I was young as the youngest son of a rice farmer.

Look if you are going to keep interrupting, we will never get started. Watch the words, count them if you must and we will see where they take us.

As I said, I was the son of a rice farmer. He had mud between his toes and mud between his ears. I, according to him and every other person in the village, had nothing but air between my ears. Everyone in the village would be breaking their backs planting rice seedlings while I listened to stories from a wandering monk.

I cared not for what any of them thought. There was a bigger world than my muddy little village and I was going to explore it.

No, it wasn't fair, but I was young and my head was full of stories and air. I didn't care. Inevitably, I ended up leaving as soon as I thought I could take care of myself. With the surprising gift of a bag of rice and a bowl to cook it in, I set out on the faint track that brought wanderers in, and very quickly after. took them away again.

The track went from muddy to earthy and the sparse trees to bamboo. It is hard to describe the exact shade of green that sunlight shining through bamboo creates, or the smell. I had never experienced either so it isn't surprising that I was paying so little attention to what I was doing that I tripped over a body lying beneath the bamboo.

At least I thought it was a body, I'd seen enough in my young life, but none with so many bandages seeping red life through them. The body moved with what I thought was miraculous speed and a knife was at my throat. I was too excited to be afraid. Here was something new, my only fear was that I would die before I took in more of this glorious experience.

Yet the knife did not cut my throat it retreated and the man sighed.

"Why should you die for my weakness?" he said, "Just be sure to bury me with all my armour."

"Why would I bury you?" I set to making a fire to cook my rice. I had heard stories of healing from the wandering monks and so, I was sure that I was a healer. I found moss and herbs and after sharing my rice with the man,

I made a poultice and put it on his wounds and make a tea for him to drink.

It is a wonder I didn't kill him, a second wonder he began to recover. The third wonder is he took me as his apprentice.

What did this man look like? I see him through two sets of eyes, the awe of youth and the weariness of the old. He was tall and strong, yet ancient (he must have been all of thirty) his armour was fearsome (it was cut and broken and mismatched).

I carried all his gear and walked behind. I tried to imitate the swagger of his walk. He made little sound and soon, I made less. When he went through his patterns with his sword, I tried to imitate him with a switch of bamboo. He laughed and corrected me, and soon he was teaching me everything he knew about the art of mayhem.

We meandered toward civilization while Hiro taught me to slice through bamboo as if I slicing through necks. It was a great game. We left the bamboo and walked through scrubby forest. We walked through a village and I ignored the fearful looks as Hiro did. In the third village, we passed one of the elders prostrated himself before Hiro.

"There are bandits troubling us, sir," he said visibly trembling. "Would you consider dealing with them for us?"

"Does it look like my honour is for sale?" Hiro said and kept walking.

"Oh no, sir," the elder shook even more as he tried to grovel and keep up with us at the same time. "But someone of your obvious honour might agree to help some poor villagers against those with none."

Hiro stopped and looked at the old man. He put his hand on his sword and appeared to be deep in thought.

"Very well," he finally said, "I need nothing, but my man here needs food and proper clothing." The old man nodded and scuttled away. I puffed out my chest at being described as a man. We waited for a while before the old man returned with some clothes that looked like they would fit and a pot filled with rice and even a bit of meat.

Hiro waved at me and I quickly changed into the new clothes. I thought they were grand, (They were thread bare dress clothes that were much too big for me.) Once the old man retreated Hiro helped himself to much of the rice and stew from the pot. Even after we both ate our fill, there was some left over.

"We must look around," Hiro said, "Watch and learn." He led me around the edge of the village and pointed out tracks where villagers went in and out of the brush. He stopped at one trail. "Look, these were made by someone wearing boots. He pointed to his own boots. I looked at my feet and saw immediately what he meant. I nodded.

We concealed ourselves and I played out battle scenarios in my head. I always came out the victor. Sometimes I slaughtered the entire evil band, and sometimes I was merciful and sent them off to become monks. I was so occupied with my inner battle that I completely missed the arrival of the bandits.

Hiro didn't. He rose on his silent feet and quietly killed the last bandit in the line of seven. Then the next, and the next. The fourth one didn't die quietly and his gurgling cry alerted the remaining three. They whirled and drew in one swift motion. Spreading out they attacked, first one, then another. Hiro was spinning and his sword whistled through the air. He was so busy defending that he didn't have time to attack.

I took a sword from one of the corpses and lunged at the back of one of Hiro's opponents. The man spun and blocked my swing with ease. He laughed and left Hiro to his two companions. He whirled his sword through the air and flicked cuts in my new clothes. Soon they were bloody rags. I heard a grunt of pain and hoped it wasn't Hiro, but I was too busy to look.

My opponent drove me back into the brush. He didn't say anything, but he was chuckling the whole time. I was no more an opponent for him than the bamboo was for me. This was a game for him, and death for me.

A root saved me. I tripped on it and fell to the ground. The bandit's sword missed its swing and caught for an instant in a branch.

I screamed and lunged again. Instead of trying to cut, I held the sword like the boar spear some of the men in the village used to kill pigs for meat. Because his sword tangled for that second, his parry was just a hair late. My sword sliced deep and cut the big artery in his thigh. Hot blood sprayed into my face and the bandit fell back with a scream.

I furiously scraped at the blood on my face trying to clear my sight. There was no sound of battle. Had Hiro won? Had the bandits? I had to see!

"It's OK, boy," Hiro's voice cut through my panic. He gave me a rag to clean my face.

When I was steadier I looked at the corpse of the bandit. If he could die then I could die too. My mortality settled around my shoulders like a cloak

"Clean your sword, then we will see if there is anything else worth taking."

"It isn't honourable to steal from the dead."

"Honour tastes good on the tongue, but it won't fill your belly," Hiro looked at me until I nodded and went over to the corpse to see what I could find.

Now if I had more time I would tell you how I almost became the best swordsman in the land, I might even tell you about the witch, but the sun is low on the horizon and I must be off.

CINDY'S FELLA

Cindy dug the shovel into the large pile of manure left behind by Cleopatra. The strong odour of the manure surrounded her and she breathed it in. Her sisters, step-sisters actually, could hardly stand to enter the barn, never mind help to clean it. Cindy loved the barn. It was her refuge from the annoyances of life in the manor house. She dumped the shovel load into the wheelbarrow and dug in for another load. It was truly astonishing how much one rather elderly cow could produce, both milk and manure. To Cindy's mind they were of equal importance.

The milk paid for the day to day expenses of the manor while the manure went to fertilize the garden patch that would feed them through the winter.

It took several trips to bring Cleopatra's contribution to the garden and properly dig it in around the vegetables, especially the large pumpkin. She was hoping to enter it in the fair. Cindy could have made just the one trip, but her step-mother didn't think it proper for her to sling the wheelbarrow around like a common farm hand. Besides it took longer this way.

Yet no matter how much she dawdled over the work, the work got done and she had to put away the tools and go back up to the house.

"Cindy," Anatolia looked up from where she lounged on the couch. "When's supper? I am famished."

"I will start it immediately," Cindy said.

"Cindy," Zetta wrinkled her nose, "You stink, I will simply not eat anything you cook before you wash."

"But I'll die if I don't eat soon." Anatolia rubbed her generous stomach.

"I doubt that very much," the girls' mother said, "Cindy go wash. You must learn to be more careful. A lady doesn't reek of the barn."

Cindy guessed she wasn't much of a lady then, since she usually reeked of the barn. She knew better than to say anything. Her step-mother wasn't too lady-like to wield a rod to chastise Cindy. Not that Cindy liked stinking to high heaven, but she saw it as an inescapable result of her efforts to feed the family.

Her family, such as it was, was otherwise completely incapable of caring for themselves. Her father had been a successful and comfortable farmer. When he died, his second wife and her daughters discovered that it took a great deal of work to be successful farmers. Work that they were completely unwilling to put in. The farm was sold off piece meal until only the large 'manor' house and barn remained with just enough land to plant a garden.

She would have liked to have soaked properly, but the threat of Anatolia's complaints drove her out the water. She dried off quickly and put her cooking dress on. It was an older mode with tighter sleeves unlikely to catch fire from the old stove.

Cindy didn't like the kitchen as much as the barn. She didn't mind cooking but there were constant interruptions.

"Is there something I can eat while I wait?" Anatolia asked as she shuffled through the narrow door. Another year and she wouldn't fit.

"There are some peeled carrots on the table," Cindy pounded on the tough meat to tenderize it enough to meet her step-mother's exacting standards.

"I don't want carrots," Anatolia whined, "Don't you have any sweets?"

"No," Cindy said, "You know your mother has banned sweets."

"And with good reason," Zetta walked in a sniffed to check on Cindy's level of cleanliness., "if you get any bigger you won't fit your dresses and Mother doesn't want to take them out again."

Anatolia picked up a carrot and heaved a great sigh. She sidled back out of the kitchen.

"Make sure you cut all the fat off my meat," Zetta said. "You missed some last night." She followed her sister out of the kitchen.

Cindy had no idea what they did with themselves through the day. They never seemed to be very far apart. Her step-mother spent her days plotting how to restore the fallen fortunes of the farm without actually going so far as to do any work. Cindy was content with the way things were. She couldn't manage a large farm by herself. Right now, she was just able to keep the balance between being busy and being able to finish her work.

She supposed some people would be upset by the demands of her step-family. But Cindy would be doing all the work anyway. After changing her dress for dinner and eating with the others she did the dishes. The last thing she did every night was milk Cleopatra.

It was dim in the barn and the old cow mooed a welcome to Cindy. She set the stool beside the cow and set the bucket in place. Cindy marveled that this last remaining cow continued to give milk in generous amounts. When the milking was done, she put the milk in the cool urn, then spent some time brushing Cleopatra. She put down fresh straw for the

cow and fill the manger with hay and the
trough with clean water.

Cindy took one last breath of the barn
air redolent with smell of everything she
loved, then closed the doors and went off to
bed.

***

She woke to the sound of the birds
singing outside her window.

"Dratted birds," she mumbled as she put
on her barn clothes and went out to milk
Cleopatra. She patted the old cow and went
through the chores. After breakfast her step-
mother sent her into town to buy a couple of
things.

"I have work to do," Cindy said.

"If I send Zetta, she will complain
bitterly," her step-mother said, "then come
back with all the wrong things to punish me.
Anatolia would just spend the money on
sweets. Get on with you." She put the few
coins into Cindy's hand. "You will take far too
long with all your talking to people, but I
know you will buy what I tell you.

So instead of working in the garden,
Cindy put on her nice dress and walked into

town. She didn't mind much. She hadn't seen her friends in a while.

"Morning, John," she said to the dairyman, "Mother wants a cheese. You can deliver it to the house later."

"Certainly, Cindy," John said, "I'll be going by that way later."

She wandered through town picking up the few things on the list from the merchants. She greeted each one by name and they treated her well though she was only spending a few pennies. In the centre of town there was a crowd gathered by a poster. Those who could read were standing near the poster and announcing its contents to everyone else.

"Hey Cindy," Bill called, "You going to the ball?"

"Do I look like I'm going to a ball?" Cindy said, "I doubt the Prince even knows I exists."

"Says here that all eligible maids are to attend the ball."

"Well then," Cindy looked at herself, "I don't look much like a maid."

The crowd laughed and Cindy waved and headed off home.

The exchange unsettled her. She enjoyed the farming, but was it what she wanted for the rest of her life? She imagined herself married to one of Bill's older brothers. They had a whole herd of milk cows and chickens too. She would be doing chores from dawn to dusk. She didn't mind the work, but there would be nothing else. Bill's mother's eulogy last year was summed up in five words. "She was a hard worker." Cindy found herself imagining what she would wear to the ball.

***

The prince stalked through the halls of the palace hoping that some servant would be foolish enough to get in his way; maybe that pert new servant girl from his mother's wing of the palace. Imagining her heart-shaped face cowed with fear made him smile. He shook his head angrily. No smiles. The prince was a person to be feared today. No one feared someone prancing about with a silly grin on their face.

Reluctantly he pushed the thought of the girl out of his head and reflected on the recent conversation with his father, the King.

"So Father," the prince had said, "Now that I'm twenty-one, are you going to make me your heir?"

"Humph," The King glowered at him and tapped his fingers on the arms of his chair. "You're too wild right now. You need to settle down and start producing heirs."

"You make me sound like some bull at one of those tiresome fairs."

The King looked the prince over and grunted, his fingers struck the wood like hammers.

"Those bulls have value," he said finally, "all you do is cause trouble. I wanted to find you a nice princess, but you've scared them all away with your antics. So, you will have to find someone from around here."

"The only women around her are farmers and servants!"

"You don't seem to find servants unattractive," the King said, "In fact your constant attraction to them is costing the kingdom a fortune. At least a farmer would be able to explain the finer points of a prize bull."

The prince swelled up to unleash his rage, but his father raised his hand.

"If you won't choose a wife, then I will choose one for you. Be sure that I will have the future needs of the kingdom in mind." The prince imagined the bride his father would select for him, some sturdy woman with a strong constitution and no grace. He shuddered.

"I am throwing a ball," The King put his hand down and ran it across the arm of his chair. "for all the maids in the kingdom. You will choose one to be your wife. When your heir is apparent, I will consider making you my formal heir."

The prince left the room very carefully not slamming the door. The King was not someone to be trifled with. As soon as he rounded the corner out of King's quarters he let his boots slam into the stone floor and twisted his face into a scowl. He was no prize bull to be set out to stud! Though to be honest, he had...collected quite a herd. He leaned against the wall and went through their faces in his mind.

***

Cindy made it back home and took the small bag of purchases into the house. She discovered her step-mother running her hands over two bolts of fine cloth.

"What did you sell this time?" Cindy asked. "I know we didn't have the money for that."

"Don't be impertinent," her step-mother's eyes took on the glare which preceded a beating., "Someone must look out for the welfare of this family."

Cindy went looking through the house trying to think of what was missing that would have paid for that cloth.

"Well, at least she won't always smell of the barn." She heard Zetta say.

"But I'll miss the fresh cream," Anatolia said.

"Cleopatra!" Cindy ran out to the barn. Sure enough, the old cow's stall was empty. She stormed back into the house and interrupted her step-mother measuring the cloth against her step-sisters.

"How could you?" Cindy said, "Cleopatra's milk was the only thing keeping us from starving."

"With a daughter married to the prince, I won't have to worry about starving."

"Every girl in the kingdom will be at that ball!"

"Which is why I had to buy the fabric; I need to give my daughters an edge."

"You could at least have bought colours that would suit them," Cindy said and ran up to her room.

She refused to come out to cook or clean. Her step-mother gave up on her and even went as far as to wedge the door closed with a chair. Anatolia came and begged her to cook. Zetta came to sneer and complain. Cindy ignored them all. She pulled out an old dress of her mother's that had hung in the back of her closet for as long as she could remember. It used to smell of her mother, now it just smelled musty.

Cindy aired the dress out and tried it on. It was loose in some places and tight in others, yet fit surprisingly well. She spent some time altering it as best she could while she tried not to hear the steady tramp of feet in and out of the house. They would never be able to pay for all this fuss. Her step-mother was going to put them out on the street. There wasn't much left to sell.

The day of the ball came and Cindy carefully rolled the dress up and fit it into a pillow case. She held the case as she climbed down the trellis outside her window. The only place she could think to change was the barn.

She put on the dress and tried her best to tidy herself.

"Well it's good to see that you can make yourself presentable," her step-mother said as she walked into the barn, "but there's no need for you to go to the ball. You have a fiancé already."

"What are you talking about?"

"Farmer Jones needs a new wife. He's had his eye on this farm for a while. Since you like farming so much, it is a perfect match. He doesn't care about this ball since he only has sons."

"Farmer Jones is old enough to be my father! I won't marry him."

"You may not like me, but I am your mother and you will do what I say."

"I won't," Cindy tried to run past her step-mother, but the older woman was faster and stronger than the she expected. She caught Cindy's arm in an iron grip and pulled her close.

"You will do what I say, girl, or some sad accident will befall you. I did it before; I can do it again." She pushed Cindy back into the barn and slammed the door closed. The bar outside dropped with a bang. All the other doors would be barred too and there was no trellis to climb down.

She felt like she was going to burst. She kicked and pounded on the door, but though it was old it was still all too solid. The sound of horses pulling a carriage came through the door and she collapsed into tears. This really was it. There was no escape from her future life as Bill's step-mother. She was younger than he was! If it had been someone else, it might have been funny.

The barn was very silent without Cleopatra in it. Cindy sighed and leaned against the door. It was going to be a long night.

She wasn't sure how long she had sat, huddled against the door before she noticed a strange light coming from Cleopatra's stall. Cindy got up to investigate. She walked to the stall and peeked around the door. Busily cleaning the stall with a tiny broom was a woman who didn't stand as tall as Cindy's waist.

"Well come in, dear," the woman said. "It isn't polite to stare."

Cindy reluctantly walked into the stall. Somehow as she entered it, the cramped space grew larger and she found herself eyeball to eyeball with the strange woman.

"Don't fret about it," the woman said, "It will just give you wrinkles." She waved her hand and a ball of light floated up above them. "Now, let me get a good look at you." She made spinning motions with her fingers and Cindy slowly turned around.

"I know that dress has sentimental value, but it just won't do." She waved her hand again and the sudden weight of a beautiful gown draped from Cindy's shoulders. She struggled to breathe.

"Small breaths, dear, a corset takes some getting used to, but you'll be fine."

She made the spinning motion with her hand again and Cindy turned again.

"Better, better." She waved her hand and Cindy's hair crawled and tugged until she thought it would pull right out.

Finally, it stopped and she lifted her hand to feel.

"Ah, ah," the woman said, "don't fuss." She led the way out into the barnyard. The moon was just rising and gave the place a magical glow. The woman walked over to the garden and peered at the pumpkin.

"This will do fine."

"But that's going to be my prize pumpkin."

"Listen, Cindy, I promised your mother to look after you, not to rescue you from your own stupidity. You can either go to the ball and marry the prince; or you can stay here, grow prize pumpkins and marry Farmer Jones."

Cindy shuddered and turned away from the garden. The woman waved her hand once more and the pumpkin exploded into a fine coach. Two unwary rabbits became horses to draw the coach, another became a driver.

"Here are the rules, child," the woman was taller than Cindy now, "You have until midnight to capture the prince; no later, not one second after midnight. At the fading of the last stroke of midnight the spell will end. Don't worry about leaving early; I've given you a little advantage. The poor boy won't be able to resist you. Just leave before the last stroke of midnight and you become the next princess. Stay any later and I won't be responsible for what happens." She smiled brightly. "But I know you will follow the rules. Now get your pretty glass slippers into the carriage and go."

Cindy climbed into the pumpkin carriage and the rabbit horses dashed away. She pulled up to the palace much sooner than she expected. More magic probably. She wondered briefly about how her mother might have met such a strange person, but she didn't have time to dwell on it. The guards helped her out of the carriage and sent it off.

"I'm supposed to leave at midnight," she said.

"That's your driver's problem," the guard said and pointed into the palace.

Cindy walked through the hallways in a daze. Torches lit the way and highlight gold framed portraits and marble sculptures. Her glass slippers clinked faintly on the stone. What would it be like to live here? She finally arrived at the doors to the ballroom. Bill stood by the door pulling at the neck of his uniform. His eyes widened when he saw Cindy.

"You look good."

"And that's a surprise?"

"No I mean you always look nice, but now you look like a princess."

"All the better to catch a prince."

"I'm not sure he's that much of a catch," Bill whispered. "Most of the girls here are terrified of him."

"So what are you doing here?"

"My father is getting married again, probably to some widow who will do nothing but complain about how the place is run. My brothers are farmers, but I want something different. This is the first step."

"So some glowing lady came and offered you the chance to change your life?"

"What are you talking about?"

"Nothing, never mind." Cindy took a deep breath. "You'd better open those doors and let me in. By the way, I'm supposed to leave at midnight. Let me know when it gets close."

"Sure thing, Cindy." Bill threw the doors open and Cindy walked into the ballroom.

The room looked like something out of a fairy tale. The walls were draped with fine cloth, a long table groaned beneath the weight of more food than Cindy's farm grew in a year. Musicians on a balcony played a sprightly tune. Though the floor had been polished to a mirror-like shine, the glass slippers gripped it comfortably. In this setting magic was easy to believe in.

Then she noticed the reek of desperation. The huge room was filled with young women who wore grim faces and glared at each other, while they shot fear filled glances at the prince. He had dressed in white and was surrounded by other men in shades of grey and black. They danced with young women while the prince lounged on the throne that had been set at the far end. He was making no attempt to hide his boredom and contempt.

It was shocking how ugly a beautiful room could be made by the presence of the wrong person. The women who should have been laughing and enjoying themselves were dressed more by their fear or avarice than their fine clothes. The men wore their lust like finery. She shuddered. Cindy was almost ready to turn around and take her chances with Farmer Jones, when her eyes met those of the prince.

***

The prince was inescapably bored. The women hovered around him. They giggled nervously or tried to act like they weren't just farmer's daughters overdressed for the night. There were two girls who wore hideous dresses, one was stuffing her face at the buffet while the other scowled at everyone who approached her. Another girl curtsied in front of him and he twirled his fingers, she stared at him.

"Turn around," he said, and rolled his eyes. She gulped and attempted a pirouette, slipped and fell to her knees, then ran off weeping. The door at the far end opened to let in some cow who couldn't tell time. He glanced up to see what new torture was to be visited upon him and his eyes met hers.

If you had put a sword to his throat he couldn't have told you the colour of her dress, but her eyes were the incredible blue of those flowers his horse ate on the side of the rode. He would never let his horse eat them again.

Without thinking about it he got up from his seat and went to greet this vision of loveliness.

Somehow his greeting turned into the first steps of a dance. The orchestra sat up straight and started playing the music for his dance. There was a collective sigh and the other girls started eyeing up his attendants in grey for possible dancing ability. Whatever dance he began she followed, she laughed at his jokes and not just a nervous titter either.

He filled her plate with food and her cup with wine. As the evening progressed he paid less and less attention to the other people who inhabited the room.

One of his guards started making odd gestures at them. He glared at the man, someone who had just joined up that day, he'd have him flogged and cast out, but only after he had finished with this most enchanting woman. He led her out to the patio where they were out of view of the crowd.

The music was quieter here, but he was content to just hum along. No conversation was necessary with those extraordinary eyes on his. He heard the clock begin to strike midnight, time to end this farce of a ball. He would marry this woman and they would rule the kingdom as soon as the old man had the decency to die.

For some reason, she was trying to pull away from him, but he was used to dealing with reluctant women and he just tightened his grip. The last stroke of midnight was fading when she shrugged and blinked.

***

The whole evening had been very strange, as if riding to a ball in an oversized pumpkin wasn't strange enough. From the moment, their eyes met the prince hadn't left her side. Cindy had watched as desperation faded to resignation and the other girls started looking for matches not quite as lofty as a prince.

He insisted on feeding her and plying her with wine. It was probably the wine that made her forget about the time. She was feeling quite tipsy by the time he pulled out onto the patio. At least there was a pleasant breeze blowing out here. The prince was humming along to the music with a fatuous grin on his face.

The clock was striking twelve. She had to leave.

Unfortunately, the prince was considerably stronger than her, and very determined that she not leave. As the clock hit the final stroke she gave up and shrugged. He would have to see what he was getting sooner or later.

The dress faded away as the sound of the clock vanished. She felt her hair tumble down to its usual tangle about her shoulders.

"What is that smell?" the prince asked.

"That would be the barn," Cindy said, "I was locked in it before all this started."

"Oh great," said the prince, "I suppose it would have been too much trouble to take a bath?"

"My step-mother locked me in the barn."

"Of course she did," the prince rolled his eyes. "Well at least let me get a decent look at you. Turn around." He waved his hand at her.

"You've been doing nothing but stare at me all night."

"But now I want to look at you."

Just her and the prince out here. The pleasant breeze of a moment ago turned chill and raised goosebumps on her arms. She crossed her arms to warm herself.

"Blast you, stupid cow!" the prince shouted, "I will see what you have." He grabbed her dress and wrenched at it. Cindy heard the fabric of her mother's dress tear and the chill wind blew across her breasts. He grabbed at her and twisted her flesh.

Cindy didn't know whether to curse herself or her mother's friend. She settled on kneeing the prince between the legs. He stopped fumbling with his pants and went a little cross-eyed.

"Guards!" he screamed. "Guards, arrest this woman!" His fists clenched and he looked like he wasn't going to wait for the guards before doing more damage. Cindy sighed and gave him a proper kick. His eyes rolled up into his head and he fell to the ground. She gathered the remnants of her dress about her and looked for an escape.

Too late. A guard approached her and stepped into the light surrounding her and the prince.

"I tried to warn you about the time," Bill said, "If I'd known what a dastard he was I would have dragged you off myself."

"So now I guess you have to arrest me." Cindy held her hands in front of her. The wind caressed her skin. Bill's eyes widened and he whipped off his vest and wrapped it around her.

"Come with me," he said his voice breaking. He put his arm around her and pulled her into the darkness as other guards came running past. None of them paid them any attention.

"Did you think the night would end like this?" Cindy said, "You throwing me into the dungeons?"

"Don't know where the dungeons are," Bill said as a familiar smell filled her nose. "I rode Blackie here when I came to work. I expect he'll be glad to carry me away again." He held her gently by the shoulders. "I'm no prince. I'm just the youngest son of an old farmer."

"Youngest sons are supposed to be lucky." Cindy put her finger on his lips. "And right now I've had my fill of princes." She helped him get Blackie out of his stall. Bill lifted her up, then jumped up behind her. Cindy could hear shouts approaching.

"I think it's time to go. I hear it's a long ride to the next kingdom."

Bill kicked Blackie into a gallop and they rode out the gates. Cindy laughed and kicked the slippers off her feet.

The tinkling sound of breaking glass followed them as they rode away into the night.

THE END OF SNOW WHITE

Snoring filled the cottage. Even with her hands tight against her ears Snow White couldn't block out the cacophony of wheezes and snorts. Chubby was worst; not because he was loudest, but because he would stop breathing for a while and, counting the seconds, she would wait until he grunted and started breathing once more.

Snow White didn't know how her grandmother had managed with seven. Maybe they hadn't snored. Maybe pigs had flown too. The only thing that had changed about the little men was their names. Snow White got up and went downstairs to clean. She might be called Snow White after her grandmother and but she didn't feel much like Snow White, more like Dingy Grey.

The truth was the little men were slobs. She used a stick to pick up the laundry. They insisted on throwing down their clothes where ever they happened to be standing when the notion took them to change from one horrifically dirty outfit to another. The sight of naked little men stomping through the cottage was seared into Snow White's mind. Nothing she said would change their behaviour. As they pointed out each time she complained, it was their cottage.

"Hey Snow," a raspy voice floated down the stairs, "You want some help getting to sleep?"

"You forget, Sleazy," Snow White said without turning around, "I've seen what you've got, and it doesn't give a girl any confidence. There's a good reason people call you 'little men'."

With a harrumph and banging of boots whichever little man it was returned to his bed. None of them were really called Sleazy, but it was the name she used whenever one of them made advances. She had learned not to turn around. She could never keep from laughing and it made them even more cantankerous than usual.

The last bit of clothing went into the huge pot she used for laundry and with a bit of soap it would do until morning. Snow White put on a cloak and went out into the night to breathe. She walked away from the cottage so none of the little men could see her. She was tired of their eyes always following her. It was cold, but the air was fresh. She amused herself by catching some of the snow that fell from the trees and comparing it with her skin. Definitely more grey than white.

"It's dangerous for a young girl to be out in the night like this." Snow White shrugged and turned to where the huntsman was stepping out of the shadows.

"It's dangerous to be me," she said, "it doesn't matter the place or time."

"Someone might come upon you and ravish you."

"Right," Snow White flipped him a hand sign that her dear departed father would have told her no self-respecting princess should know never mind employ. Sorry, Pops, she thought, I've got no respect left, for myself or anyone else.

The huntsman frowned and gripped her shoulder.

"I have the power of life and death over you, Princess," he said.

"Sure," Snow White said, "You could go running to your Queen and tell her that you accidentally didn't really kill me, and sort of accidentally brought her a deer heart instead."

The huntsman growled and gripped her tighter, he put a hand on the collar of her dress and Snow White stopped him.

"Don't you dare rip my dress." She pushed him away, "This is the last bit of comfortable clothing I have left."

"But..." The huntsman pouted.

"Oh, alright," Snow White said, and let her dress fall to the snow, "Just pretend my cloak is my dress. But can we please at least go somewhere dry? There's a cave this way." She picked up the dress and led the Huntsman deeper into the woods.

In the morning Snow White watched the little men stagger off toward the mine that gave them just enough iron ore to eke out a living. Adding her full-sized appetite to the mix really stretched their resources. That was why she pretended that she didn't know that they doubled back to watch her take her bath and wash her clothes. For people who made so much noise the rest of the time, they were remarkably quiet.

As punishment for the come-on the night before, Snow White cut short her washing and wrapped up in a towel that felt like burlap. She boiled some water and tossed in some mint for flavour. She sat in the kitchen and waited for her clothes to dry enough to get dressed. It was a once a week ritual that no one talked about. One of these days they would make the connection between the midnight propositions and the length of her bath. She snorted, probably not. Little they were, but they were still men.

Snow White sipped her mint tea and considered her life. The huntsman was mildly amusing, but his obsession with her was going to cause trouble. It was the same with all of them. They all thought that they were beyond the sight of the Queen. The end was always the same. At least her father had just thrown them in the dungeons. The Queen apparently was infuriated by the ease with which Snow White ensnared the boys and men around her. The men in Snow White's life tended to die. It was depressing.

The Queen wanted Snow White dead, and Snow White didn't blame her. But she wasn't going to lie down and die for anyone. She wasn't enjoying her life much, but she wasn't ready to give it up just yet.

"Are you sure you'll be alright?" Chubby looked up at Snow White. "I'll stay here and take care of you while the others go to town."

"Sure," said Handy, "and we all know what you'll be about while we're gone." He glowered at the other four little men. "We all go. She'll be just fine." He looked up at her through his eyebrows. Snow White nodded and that was that. The little men clambered up on the wagon, and their one wretched mule pulled them away down the trail away from the cottage. Snow White watched long enough to be sure that they were gone. She could count on their jealously to keep them all together to town and back.

Snow White heated the water and luxuriated in the first long, private bath in months. She almost wished the huntsman would come by.

Snow White washed all the linens and scrubbed what she could of the cottage. She hated cleaning, but she hated dirt worse. The days passed and she found herself missing the company. They were pigs and perverts and whatever else, but they surrounded her with life. Snow White wasn't very good company for herself.

The huntsman never showed and when the little men came home she learned why.

"The Queen had him him tied to a stake and then choked him with his own organ."

"How could she choke him with his heart?" she said.

"It wasn't his heart," Handy said, "It was a different organ."

"Right," Snow White said, "so what did you buy for food?"

"The usual," Chubby said. Snow White rolled her eyes. "If we bought anything different the Queen would suspect something.

"Why would she care about a few grubby miners?"

"She cared about the huntsman sure enough," Pinky said.

Snow White shrugged.

"You don't seem too upset that a man who saved your life is dead." Handy said.

"Every man in my life ends up dead," Snow White said, "It's like a curse." She laughed as the little men all backed away from her. "Dinner isn't going to cook itself." She walked into the cottage. "I'll call you when it's ready," she said over her shoulder.

The little men kept their distance for a day or two, but habit and inclination were too strong and soon they were ogling her again and strutting naked through the cottage. Their raspy voices called from the top of the stairs at night. Snow White went from feeling dingy grey to feeling very dark indeed.

Their snores still kept her awake; but something was different tonight. The sound didn't have its full richness. A small man climbed into her bed and grabbed at her flesh.

"Don't pretend you don't like it," the little man said, "You went off quick enough with your precious huntsman." Snow White made a noise of disgust and pushed the little man away. She pulled her legs up to her chest. "So now you go all shy and virtuous," the man sneered and tried to push her legs aside. Snow

White kicked out and launched the little man out of the bed. He bounced across the floor and down the stairs.

The snores of the other little men didn't change. Snow White didn't feel like going and dealing with whoever was at the bottom of the stairs. With any luck, he would just go back to bed and try to forget his humiliation.

When the men got up in the morning, they found Handy lying at the bottom of the stairs with his neck broken. They looked at him, then Snow White who stood at the top of the stairs.

"Well, damn," Chubby said, "How are we going to survive with just four of us running the mine?" They all turned and looked at Snow White.

"No," she said, "no way. I'm no miner."

"You're going to earn your keep one way or another," Chubby said. "You choose."

"If I bang my head," she said, "I'm going to burn your supper."

Pinky went up the stairs and fetched Handy's work bag. He handed her the dead man's helmet and pick axe. The four little men picked up their comrade and slung him on the wagon. Snow White followed them to the mine.

They tossed the body into a dead-end tunnel and piled some rocks to block it. One of them spat on the rocks then they led Snow White deeper into the mine. She saw a glint in the rock from one of their lamps. She turned her own lamp on the rock.

"Is this gold?" she said.

"Yup," Chubby said, "Leave it alone."

"Why?"

"What would happen if someone learned we had gold up here? They'd come and kill us and take our mine, that's what would happen. Gold is trouble. Stick to the iron ore."

Snow White shook her head, but the little men didn't look so ridiculous with their hammers and axes. They led her deep into the mountain. She banged her head several times and muttered curses that bounced off the little men. They were in their element now. The cottage was only where they lived. The mine was where they were alive.

She hated it. Even with the helmet her head ached. Soon, her shoulders and back ached too. The little men cracked the rock with hard, rhythmic strokes. Snow White's hands vibrated from hitting the rock and she barely scratched the surface.

"OK," Chubby said after an eternity, "Go and make us supper."

The walk back to the cottage was long and excruciating. It was worse than the night that she had followed the huntsman into the woods knowing that she would have to seduce him to save her life. She couldn't face the idea of seducing the little men. The very idea made her ill.

Even the snoring didn't keep her awake that night or for the rest of the week. She slept exhausted until morning. The men glared at each other jealously. Snow White knew it was only a matter of time before they came up with a solution that would make them happy and complete her fall from being Snow White.

It didn't take as long as she had hoped.

"I got the short straw," Pinky said and leered at her.

"Short straw," said Snow White, "how appropriate." His leer slipped a little, but only a little. The work day passed as slowly as all the others. Snow White walked back to the cottage as quickly as she could. She could pack up and move on. She didn't know where, but she would find a place.

The berries were lit by a beam of golden sunlight. The huntsman had pointed them out once.

"Eat one of those and you'll never wake up," he'd said.

Snow White looked at them. Here was her solution. She thought of sleeping and never waking up. After picking every berry there she hurried back to the cottage. She crushed the berries and added them to the rough stew that was all they ate. It smelled as vile as it always did. Her cooking was only marginally better than the little men's.

The little men arrived home. They came to the table with their filthy hands and filthier grins. They were all looking forward to this night. The stew vanished from their plates and Snow White dished out seconds. Finally, Pinky sighed and let out a huge belch.

"Well boys," he said, "I'm for bed." He winked at them and leered at Snow White. "Don't keep me waiting."

"I'll just clean up some," Snow White said.

"Don't keep me waiting," Pinky said again and let his hand rest on her shoulder possessively. Snow White nodded.

She heard them stomping around upstairs. She took as long as she could clearing up.

"Get up here, girl," the raspy voice of a little man came down the stairs. Snow White took a deep breath and slowly climbed the stairs. The four men were staring at her.

"Well," Pinky said as he stood naked and eager, "it's time." Then he fell flat on his face and started snoring. The others fell back on their beds and began snoring too.

Snow White stood there and listened to the snores. She listened until one by one the snores stopped.

In the morning, she took the wagon and the old mule. She left the bodies in the beds. It took her all day to load the loose gold at the mine into the wagon.

"Let's go," she said to the mule. "One last trip and you can retire." She drove the mule away from the mine and the cottage and the last of the Kingdom that knew her as Princess Snow White.

She looked at her arms that were black with rock dust, maybe someday she would feel clean again.

OTHER BOOKS BY ALEX

Calliope and the Sea Serpent
Wendigo Whispers
The Devil Reversed
Generation Gap
The Gods Above
Tales of Light and Dark
Like Mushrooms (poetry and
photography)
The Heronmaster
Blood and Sparkles, and other stories
Princess of Boring
By the Book
Sarcasm is My Superpower
Playing on Yggdrasil
The Unenchanted Princess

Alex also has stories in:

Words on the Rocks
Beyond the Wail
Collidor Stream Collection 2016

CPSIA information can be obtained
at www.ICGtesting.com
Printed in the USA
BVHW030933041221
623217BV00002B/124

9 781775 128649